How to be a
Heartbreaker

Codi Gary

Crazy for You
Copyright © 2016 by Codi Gary
ISBN-13: 978-1542547710
ISBN-10: 1542547717

NYLA Publishing
350 7th Avenue, Suite 2003, NY 10001, New York.
http://www.nyliterary.com

Dedication

To My Sister from another Mister.

I love you, Tina.

1

Rule #7- Never kiss and tell.

Sebastian Valentine turned his Audi R8 down the mountainside road, gazing out over the valley where Promise, Idaho lay nestled amidst the jagged Sawtooth Mountains. A town of only 4,500 people during the farming seasons and less once winter set in, Bash remembered the stifling small town atmosphere had driven him to Hollywood when he was just eighteen. But looking down on it now, a warm glow spread through his chest, a sense of coming home that he'd never thought he'd experience.

As he reached the bottom and headed down the main road through town, he couldn't believe how little had changed in twelve years. A few of the buildings might have had a new paint job, and it looked like old Doc Fergusson had updated the Promise Medical Clinic on Sycamore, but other than that, it was exactly the same.

Bash hoped at least the people had evolved.

He followed the commands of his GPS, taking him to the new vacation home he'd bought just outside of town. Most of his friends from L.A. chose to stay in Sun Valley, about twenty minutes away, but it hadn't made sense for him. Not when his best friend, Troy Jenkins, was here.

And his father, of course, but Bash hadn't seen his dad, Samuel, since the night he'd kicked him out. As far as he knew, his dad still lived above the car garage he'd worked at for thirty years. Would he be happy to know Bash had bought a house in town, even if it was only for breaks between projects? He doubted it. The stubborn son of a bitch would probably be the first one to tell him to get his ass out of there.

His hands-free rang through his radio, indicating he had a call coming in. He saw Troy's name on the screen and said, "Answer."

"Hey, you here yet?" Troy practically yelled through the speaker.

"Yeah, just finding my house now."

"Sweet, call me when you get settled! We're going out tonight! Woooo hoooo!"

"Alright, I'll call you in a little while."

"Later."

Bash chuckled at Troy's excitement. The two of them had been friends since Kindergarten, and even though Troy's father owned the local pharmacy, and Bash's dad was a roughneck mechanic with a bad temper, they had remained close through ups and downs. When Bash had been sent away at sixteen to spend six months at a boys camp in Montana, Troy had called and written him every week.

2

The funny thing was that besides Troy, that stay at Saddle Creek Boys Ranch was one of the best memories he had of growing up. John Stone, the owner, had been the first adult to ever treat him like he could be more than a greaser's kid.

It was why the call a week ago from Rayne McCoy, letting him know about John's stroke, had hit him so hard. He'd dropped everything to fly out to Saddle Creek, Montana and pay his respects to the greatest man he'd ever known. John hadn't regained consciousness during the few days he'd stayed, but it had still been the right thing to do.

Instead of flying back to L.A., he'd bought the Audi and driven across two states to see his new house. The delivery truck was supposed to arrive at two with his bed, furniture, and clothing for the month, and the Internet and phone were being hooked up today.

Bash pulled up the driveway to his new place, a charming gray two-story ranch house with a wraparound porch and a large swing in the front yard. Not that he needed the swing for anything, but it made the house look idyllic, homier—which was something he craved, even if he wasn't willing to say it out loud. He wanted the perfect life, and he'd gotten it. As one of the most sought after action movie stars, he had more money than he'd ever dreamed of, and never wanted for anything. He dated the most beautiful women, and ended it when they started getting too attached.

It wasn't bad for a poor kid from a Podunk town in Idaho.

He climbed out of his Audi and looked around his place. It used to be owned by Promise Farms, one of the biggest outfits in town, but they'd been struggling the last few years and needed to sell off some of their assets. There was a detached four-car garage next to the house, and a large shop in the back. Ten acres of green grass and trees stretched out behind, but on the right he could see clearly into his neighbor's front yard.

Bash stopped in mid-stride as he caught sight of a woman standing on the front porch of the neighboring house. He didn't recognize her with the large, dark sunglasses, but she appeared to be watching him.

He waved to be friendly, and she slid her glasses up onto the top of her head…

And flipped him the bird.

Bash was sure he was seeing things, but nope, that middle finger was definitely directed at him.

Before he could decide if he should head over and find out what the hell her problem was, she turned around and walked inside. Loud barking erupted where the woman had just stood and Bash watched in horror as a giant black hairy beast started running toward him.

Bash ran toward the front porch of the house, keeping an eye on the dog. The whole scene seemed to play out in slow motion and Bash swore he could see ropes of saliva flying from the dog's massive lips as he gained ground.

It occurred to Bash as he leaped for the door that he didn't have a key to the house yet, since the realtor was supposed to meet him there at one and he was a little early. He prayed luck was on his side and the door was unlocked; otherwise, he was gonna be dog chow.

The doorknob didn't turn, and Bash put his back to the solid wood, closing his eyes as he waited for the massive canine to sink his fangs into his throat.

When something slammed into his balls instead, Bash bent over with a cry of pain and found the dog's head buried in his crotch, all hot breath and wet nose.

Realizing that the dog probably wasn't planning to chomp down on his testicles, he reached down and tried to pull him away from the front of his pants.

"Okay, dude, I know I probably smell awesome, but you should at least buy me dinner first."

"That is pretty disgusting," a feminine voice said.

Bash looked up, and found the woman from the porch standing at the bottom of his steps, holding a black leash.

"Propositioning my dog? I knew some of you Hollywood types had weird fetishes, but didn't know *you* were into that."

Bash stopped struggling with the dog. "I wasn't, I was joking."

"With who? Bernie? I hate to tell you this but no matter what the movies portray, dogs actually don't speak English."

Giving her the lopsided grin Oprah had called "irresistible," he said, "You know, most of the time I at least know someone's name when they're insulting me."

"You already know my name, jackass. Bernie, come."

The dog whipped his head around, abandoning his treasure, and loped down the steps to sit in front of her. She snapped the leash

5

on him without so much as another glance in Bash's direction, and it irked him.

Bash studied her, trying to place the high cheekbones and long dark hair pulled back from her face. She had a pretty face—tan and slightly freckled, with deep brown eyes. In a sleeveless shirt and a pair of denim shorts that showed off legs for days, she was striking.

And yet, he still had no idea who she was or why she was so pissed at him.

"I actually don't. Sorry."

She had just started walking back to her place, but when he spoke she paused and faced him with a terrifying expression. "Really? Well, just Google Sebastian Valentine fucks Fatty. Maybe it will jog your memory."

What the hell? He had only slept with a handful of girls from Promise and none of them had been—

Bash stilled as he stared after the woman's hourglass figure and heart shaped ass.

There was only one woman he'd known in Promise whom people had ever called fat, out of sheer stupidity, but he couldn't think of one single reason for Ashlynn Marks to be pissed at him.

2

Ashlynn Marks wasn't the violent sort, but seeing Sebastian Valentine looking just as sexy at thirty as he had at eighteen made her a little homicidal.

And the jerk didn't even remember her name? He'd ruined *her life* and yet he couldn't be bothered to actually feel bad that he'd screwed her brains out in the back of his piece of shit Impala and let one of his dirtbag friends take pictures? Not to mention that when she'd gone by his place to confront him the next day, she'd found out he'd skipped town without saying a word.

Her first time having sex and the whole event had been catalogued with shots of them in various positions and poses. The posters had been spread about town, on bulletin boards and stapled on the outside of businesses. It had been humiliating, and Sebastian hadn't even had the decency to stick around to enjoy the aftermath.

At least he could have waited until she had a chance to break his nose.

Fine, so she was being dramatic. It had been twelve years, and frankly, people hardly remembered the day after it had happened.

But now, he was back and all of this shit was going to come up again. Hell, he was living next door. Their driveways were a few hundred feet from each other and there would be no avoiding him in a town this small.

Plus, it didn't help that their best friends were marrying each other. Maggie Thomas, the bride to be, had assured Ashlynn that even though Sebastian had bought himself a whole freaking *house*, he was only there for the wedding festivities and then he'd be going back to his life of movies and size zero models. It was a vacation home, but what kind of movie stars went on vacation in Promise? Which was perfect for Ashlynn; the less she had to see of his stupid face the better.

Pulling Bernie inside the house, she heard her landline ringing and rushed in to answer.

"Hello?"

"Dr. Marks? It's Rosa Winters, and I've got a serious problem."

Ashlynn nearly sighed aloud. Taking over the town's medical practice had been her dream, but as one of only two doctors, she also had to take calls during her lunch and sometimes after hours. And lucky her, at least three of her patients were overzealous hypochondriacs.

Like Mrs. Rosa Winters.

"Of course, Mrs. Winters, what seems to be the problem?"

"I was just in the bathroom, trying to pee, and I felt this horrible pain in my...well, my girly parts. Do you think it could be cancer?"

"You know, Rosa, I doubt it since you just had a pap smear a few months ago and were fit as a fiddle, but why don't you come by the clinic in an hour and I'll run a few tests." It was the only way to stop Rosa from blowing up her phone all night long while she was out with her girls. They had been planning this celebration for Karianne Paulsen since she found out she was going to be the new principle at Promise Elementary School. So many big changes for their threesome; Maggie getting married, Karianne becoming the youngest principle in the history of the school and Ashlynn taking over the practice...it was almost bitter sweet.

"Thank you for doing this, Dr. Marks."

Rosa's gratitude pulled her out of her melancholy. "Of course, Rosa, see you soon."

Ashlynn hung up the phone and went to the kitchen to make her lunch, trying not to let her new neighbor and the changes coming stress her out. Tonight would be the first time her new associate, Trevor Grimes, covered the afterhours shift at the clinic. Although the nearest hospital was only thirty minutes away, Ashlynn had wanted to create a closer alternative for the people of Promise. A lot of them were older and terrified of hospitals, so a twenty-four-hour clinic was something she had been longing to do, but she'd needed to find the right person. She and Trevor had gone to medical school together and when she'd mentioned looking for an associate, he'd jumped on board.

While she pulled all the sandwich fixings from the fridge, she couldn't help but stare across the way to where Sebastian walked off the steps, holding his arms out to Cate Herman, local realtor and one of Ashlynn's high school tormentors… who had graduated into her adult tormentor, but in a subtler way. Instead of Twinkies taped to her locker or a wide load sign on her back, Cate liked to make little digs at her in that syrupy sweet tone Ashlynn loathed.

As the two of them embraced, Ashlynn felt a little bile rise up in her throat. When they pulled back, she couldn't help mimicking Cate aloud.

"Oh, Sebastian, you're so rich and handsome and I'm a gold digging whore. Wouldn't you love to have sex with me? I promise to tell you I'm on the pill, but really, I'm not."

Sebastian ran his hair through his short, brown hair and whatever he said made Cate laugh and stroke his arm.

"Ugh," Ashlynn groaned, turning her back on the window.

Forgetting her sandwich for a moment, she went to the pink pig cookie jar on the counter and pulled two chocolate chip cookies from it. One was halfway shoved into her mouth when she turned to find Bernie with both of his huge paws on the counter and her container of turkey in his mouth.

"Bernie, you greedy bastard!"

He dropped the turkey and took off to the other room. Ashlynn inspected the container while eating her other cookie and her stomach turned at the slimy, string of drool he left behind on the plastic.

"God, you are disgusting."

Finishing the chocolaty goodness, she washed the container, noting there were no holes. She caught sight of Bernie in the entryway, his black bushy tail waving back and forth like he just didn't care.

"You're lucky I foiled your evil plan or you would have been in big trouble."

He let loose with a string of booming barks, and she suddenly realized she was talking to her dog. The same thing she'd mocked Sebastian for doing not ten minutes ago.

It's okay if you do it, it's your dog.

Her cell phone buzzed, and she slid the answer button below Maggie's name and tapped the speakerphone icon.

"Hello?"

"So, have you seen him yet?"

Ashlynn took a bite of her turkey on whole wheat, looking out the window for Sebastian and Cate, but they were nowhere to be seen.

"Unfortunately."

"Well, what did he say? What did you say? Did he apologize for the pictures?" Maggie asked in that rapid-fire voice of hers.

"He said something stupid, and I called him a jackass, and no, he didn't even know who I was."

"What?" Maggie yelled, her voice echoing through the kitchen. "How the hell did he not remember you? What an asshole! I don't care that he is Troy's best friend, this seriously makes me question my love for him."

Ashlynn heard Troy's affronted, "Hey," in the background and rolled her eyes. "Shut up, you know you adore Troy. It's not his fault his friend is a devil in expensive clothing."

"Okay, but be honest…he's pretty hot, right?"

Ashlynn would admit no such thing. She would not confess to checking out that muscular build, or avoiding his incredible blue eyes because of their irresistible magnetic pull.

God, she was pathetic. After everything he'd done and everything she knew him to be, she still mooned after him like that lovesick girl who'd sported the huge crush on her savior.

"Yes, he's still a good looking guy, but that's how he reels you in. Makes you fall for the champion of the weak and unpopular, and then he kisses you until your toes curl and bam, he leaves town. Nothing. Nada. Zip for twelve years. And then, when he does show up and happens to be your neighbor, he doesn't even remember your name."

"So, you're not bitter or angry at all. Good to know," Maggie said dryly.

"Is this the only reason you called?"

"No, it is not. I also want to make sure you show up in something hot tonight, and not just jeans and a t-shirt. We're celebrating, which means dressed to the nines with heels, a boob shirt, and if I see a scrunchie, I will not be responsible for my actions."

"Whoa, you're kind of being a dictator…emphasis on the dick," Ashlynn said.

12

"Is it too much to ask that on a night out with my girls I don't feel like you're ready to bail at any minute to go home and stream some stupid comedy and cuddle with that disgusting dog of yours?"

"She doesn't mean it, Bernie," Ashlynn crooned. Bernie lifted his head from where it had been lying on his paws and cocked it to the side.

"See, and you're talking to him now. You need to get out of that house, away from all your crazy patients, get drunk and possibly make out with a sexy guy who will knock your socks, pants and underwear off!"

"Maggie, let me make this very clear." Taking a huge bite of her turkey sandwich and chewing it slowly, she could hear the impatience vibrating through the phone.

"Did you put me on mute or something?" Maggie called.

"Nope, was chewing my lunch, but if I get even the slightest suspicion that you're trying to set me up tonight, I know a hundred ways to murder you and make it look natural. So, whoever you told to show up tonight, you better call and cancel."

"Why? You're a single adult in need of some serious loosening up. Why not let your freak flag fly?"

"Because that's how naked pictures of me ended up plastered all over town."

3

Bash stood at the bar with Troy and a few more friends, nursing a whiskey as he watched the people inside Broken Promises Saloon. Well, technically, he watched one woman in particular.

Ashlynn swayed to the beat of a Brantley Gilbert song, her long dark hair like a chocolate waterfall around her shoulders. She laughed at something Troy's fiancé, Maggie, did. The tiny redhead with curls like Shirley Temple was cute, nice, and Troy obviously adored her. Maggie had at least come over to kiss Troy and say hi.

Her friends, however, hadn't even addressed Bash when they'd walked through the door, Ashlynn in her white halter top, jean skirt, and brown cowboy boots. She'd come up to the bar and bought three shots for herself, Maggie, and their other friend, Karianne, before shooting them back and heading out onto the dance floor. Karianne, who had champagne blond hair and a set of hard green eyes, had glared daggers at him as Ashlynn pulled her along by the hand.

Troy had filled him in on why Ashlynn hated his guts, but he still hadn't figured out the right way to talk to her. To explain that he'd had no idea the two of them were being photographed and if he had, he would have climbed out of the car and beat the shit out the culprit. He had never been the guy to kiss and tell, and he would especially not have done anything to hurt or embarrass Ashlynn.

It was still hard for him to associate the strong, vivacious woman on the dance floor with the shy, curvy girl he remembered. The one who had been paired with him when she was a freshman and he was a junior on their Biology project. He'd hated school and was ready to be done, but having just returned from Saddle Creek, he was determined to at least graduate. John, the man who'd run the boys camp, had taught him a lot in those six months. About respecting himself enough to do what was right for him and protecting people who couldn't do it themselves.

He'd given all the boys at the camp a list of rules, and Bash had tried to live by them as best he could. And talking about your conquests was definitely a violation of John's teachings.

Which was why Bash had never said a word about that night after he'd finally graduated high school, when he'd come upon Ashlynn, who was a sophomore, surrounded by a group of guys from their school. She'd been struggling not to cry, he could tell by the set of her shoulders and the sheen of tears in her eyes.

"What's the matter, chunk? No smart-ass comment now? Huh? Not gonna call me dumb?" Paul Jacobs was the same age as Bash and was leaving Promise behind with a full-ride football scholarship to some school in Florida. Bash had always thought he

was a prick with a massive ego, but had never thought he'd be the type to gang up on one girl.

Ashlynn didn't say a word, just kept backing away as the circle closed in.

Paul grabbed her arm and pulled her up against him. That seemed to wake her up and she started struggling.

"I think you should make it up to me. Apologize properly."

All of it happened fast, and before he knew what he was about to do, Bash stepped out of the shadows. *"You're going to let her go. Now."*

"Whoa, hey man! Where did you go?" Troy asked, pulling Bash out of the past.

"Nowhere, just thinking about what I'm going to say to get Ashlynn to talk to me."

Troy shook his head. "I would just let it go if I were you. She's been stewing on her hatred of you for a long ass time. No way is an explanation gonna disintegrate all that."

Bash finished off his glass of whiskey with a hiss. "Even if I'm innocent?"

"Especially that. Otherwise, she has no one to blame anymore except the unknown prick who took the pictures."

Bash had gone searching for the pictures last night after the Wi-Fi had been hooked up at his place and he had to say, they weren't even that clear, which was probably why he'd never seen them before. Most of them were of the back of his head, except that one of his bare ass, but even that was fuzzy.

He still couldn't figure out how someone had taken a picture of them without the flash going off. He hoped at least if a big white light had flashed through the window, he would have noticed.

Then again, he had been a little busy.

The girls came back over to the bar, and Bash stepped forward, about to ask to buy Ashlynn a drink, when another man slid in beside her. He reminded Bash of Toby Keith, a blond giant with big teeth and curly hair to his shoulders.

"Hey there, Ash. Can I buy you a drink?"

Bash knew the guy, but couldn't place him until Ashlynn called him Nick.

Nick the Dick. And the nickname wasn't for his attitude.

"Sure, Nick. You know I never turn down free booze," Ashlynn said.

Nick had been the year behind him, but had played varsity football since he was a freshman, due to his size. The guy was still built like a brick wall, but had always been a good guy. At least, from what Bash remembered of him.

"How's it going, Nick?" Bash asked.

Nick turned to see who was talking to him and his eyes widened. "Holy shit! Sebastian Valentine!" Nick held out his hand and when Bash took it, he found himself brought into a big hug against Nick's massive chest. "It is good to see you."

Bash finally pulled back and caught Ashlynn's look of disgust. At least she wasn't pretending he was invisible anymore.

"Thanks, you too, man," Bash said.

"I've got all your movies! You are awesome. Hey, what was it like to work with Bruce Willis? I saw him once when I was delivering in Sun Valley, but I couldn't even talk!"

"Delivering?" Bash asked.

"Oh, yeah, I work for FedEx. Man, I can't believe you're here!"

Nick handed Ashlynn her shot without even looking, his attention on Bash, while Bash watched Ashlynn glare at the back of Nick's head.

"Well, Bruce is a real professional guy, easy to work with," Bash said.

Ashlynn finished her shot and slipped her arm through Nick's. "Hey Nick, do you wanna dance?"

"In a minute, Ash."

This time, Ashlynn's glare was directed at Bash as she headed back onto the dance floor, her friends close behind. Bash's gaze followed the way that short jean skirt twitched back and forth, and he decided then and there that before the night was through, he was going to have a little talk with Ashlynn.

"So, tell me more about being an action star. Do you do all your own stunts?" Nick asked.

Just as soon as he could shake his new super fan.

***

Ashlynn was six shots in and feeling really good. Besides the few encounters with Sebastian she couldn't ignore, she was actually having a blast just dancing with her girls, forgetting about all her stress and responsibilities.

"Want another shot?" Karianne asked.

"Woo hooo, shots!" Maggie shouted.

Troy had agreed to take them all home at the end of the night, so they were all pretty hammered, and Ashlynn's common sense tried to break through the haze of alcohol.

If you have another one, you're going to be hugging the porcelain goddess tomorrow.

But three sheets to the wind Ashlynn cheered, "More shots!"

The three of them danced their way through the crowd of people who had filled up Broken Promises Bar in the last few hours until Maggie threw her arms around Troy, who was leaning against the bar with his friends.

"Whoa, you having fun, babe?" he asked.

"Yes. I just love you so much. 'Cause you are gonna be my husband." Her voice was high and singsongy and Ashlynn made a face when Troy kissed Maggie sweetly on the lips.

"What's up, you don't like Troy?" Sebastian asked next to her.

Where the hell had he come from? Ashlynn turned toward him with her arms crossed. "What are you talking about?"

"You were making a face at them, and I asked if you didn't like Troy."

"Of course I like Troy. He's a good guy. I just don't like his taste in friends," Ashlynn said.

"Come on, Ash, let's get the shots," Karianne said.

Sebastian stepped in front of Ashlynn before she could move. "I think the two of us need to have a conversation. I know what you think I did, but I had no idea anyone was taking pictures."

"Whatever, I don't even care anymore, it was so long ago," she lied.

"Then why are you acting as if I'm the anti-Christ? If you'll just let me explain—"

"Or you could just stay the hell away from me, and we'll be all good."

Sebastian's beautiful mouth thinned into an angry line. "Have it your way."

He walked away from her toward the entrance, and Ashlynn found herself chasing after him, ignoring her friends calling her name behind her. She stepped out onto the wooden steps and saw him opening up the door to his car.

"So, you're going to take off again without a word?"

Sebastian paused halfway into his car and looked up at her. "I'm just going home."

"Yeah, I'm sure." Ashlynn had no idea why she was pushing him like this, especially when she'd told him to leave her alone, but when he slammed his door and started marching back up to stand toe to toe with her, her world spun a bit.

Whoa, was he always so tall?

"That night, after we finished and I drove you home, you said *thank you*, and got out of my car without giving me a phone number or anything. And then, I got home and my old man and I got into it and he kicked me out. So, I left town a little earlier than I'd planned

20

and I had no idea that the girl who had practically jumped out of my car to get away from me actually wanted me to call her."

Ashlynn didn't remember it that way at all. She'd remembered awkwardly getting dressed, and listening to him talk about getting the hell out of this town. Her heart had sunk deeper with every word as she realized that she'd just had sex with the guy she'd been crushing on for two years and he couldn't wait to get away from her.

Humiliated, she'd barely been able to manage that quiet *thank you* before she'd started balling her eyes out. She'd run into her house and broken down across her bed, heaving sobs into her pillow.

And then the next day, her tears had given way to fury.

"You kept talking about leaving town, so I figured that was it. I didn't know that I wasn't even going to warrant a good-bye."

"I was an eighteen-year-old kid! I'm sorry I hurt your feelings, but I had my own shit going on," he said.

"You're such a jerk." The shout cost her dearly as her stomach started to turn. Bile rose up in her throat and before she could stop it, she was bent over and vomiting.

Right on top of his shoes.

"Shit." He jumped back out of sight, and she continued to heave, tears gathering in her eyes, blinding her. Someone had taken her hair into their hand and was rubbing her back softly, murmuring. She realized it was Sebastian and she wanted to scream at him to stop being nice to her, but couldn't speak.

Sucking in air, she decided that if she was going to be struck by lightning and die swiftly, this would be the time.

21

And then she wasn't thinking at all as she pitched forward and proceeded to pass out.

4

Bash grimaced at the squish of vomit under his feet as he carried Ashlynn down the steps and placed her into the passenger seat of his car. This wasn't exactly how he'd imagined his first night back in Promise ending. He'd figured maybe he'd explain to Ashlynn what happened, and then it would be on her to accept the truth.

He hadn't expected her to blow up and chase him down. Never dreamed she'd vomit on his thousand dollar shoes.

And he especially hadn't expected to be driving a passed out Ashlynn home. He'd texted Troy to let him know she was with him, and then turned up his classic rock station, trying to drown out his busy brain.

What had he been thinking trying to talk to her when she was shit-faced? Hell, she probably wouldn't remember half of what he'd said in the morning.

He pulled into her driveway ten minutes later, and when he lifted her into his arms, he smelled the rancid scent of vomit. Jesus, had she puked on herself? He was going to have to clean her up. There was no putting her to bed in the clothes she was in.

The sound of deep baying came from inside the house, and Bash realized that her giant ball-butting dog was just waiting for them the minute he opened the door.

Damn it. Would the dog freak out and attack him if he caught him carrying his mistress?

Making a crazy decision, Bash put Ashlynn back in his car and drove back out and into his driveway. He wasn't fully unpacked, but at least he wouldn't get mauled for being a good guy.

He managed to unlock the door and carry Ashlynn inside, kicking his soiled shoes off. He took her up the stairs to his bedroom.

When he flipped on the light, she mumbled a bit, but didn't stir. He could see the stain on the front of her white halter and fought his own urge to puke.

God, this was going to be a fucking mess. Would it be wrong if he set her on the floor to change her?

He decided that if he could just keep her on her back, it should be fine.

Laying her on top of his bed, he left for a second to get a towel, a warm wet washcloth, and grabbed a t-shirt out of his dresser as he came back into the room. He laid the towel on the ground and took off his socks and pants, starting a pile of dirty clothes on top.

Ashlynn hadn't moved, her hair fanned out in a tangled mess around her head. He wiped around her mouth and chin, but then she groaned and tried to turn on her side.

"Stop licking me, Bernie," she mumbled.

Bash stopped his ministrations, laughing quietly at being mistaken for her dog, and dropped the washcloth on the towel. He had gotten her face clean anyway, but now he could see that even her skirt had droplets of vomit.

There was no leaving her in her clothes—at least, not in his bed. Kneeling in front of her, Bash pulled off her boots and socks first, and then, with a deep breath, reached for the snap of her skirt.

He jumped when she grabbed his hand weakly, and he peered up to find her sitting up slightly, watching him with half closed eyes.

"What'sa doin'? she slurred.

"I was just trying to get you changed. Your clothes are covered in puke."

"Oh. Sanks." She flopped back on the bed and he waited for a second until he heard a soft snore.

Well, at least she'd acknowledged she knew what was going on. That had to lessen the creep factor a bit, since getting her out of her filthy clothes was still a necessity, if he didn't want to be cleaning puke off his bed tomorrow. He pulled her skirt down the length of her legs before he changed his mind, trying not to look at her pink lacy panties. Jesus, what the hell was wrong with him? He fished her keys and phone out of her pockets and set them on the nightstand.

Finally, he just had the halter top to go, and he had no idea why his palms were sweating so much. He was careful as he lifted her into a sitting position and untied the halter strings behind her neck.

When he'd wrestled the halter up and dropped it onto the towel, he was left with one last conundrum. Did he remove her bra or was that going too far? The thing looked uncomfortable, if the way her breasts pushed up over the top was any indication.

Ah, hell, stop looking at her chest, asshole.

Bash pulled the t-shirt on over her head, and when he had it in place, lifted her again. He pushed the back of the t-shirt up and unsnapped the strapless bra, throwing it on top of the pile of soiled clothes.

Once he had her under the covers of his bed, he went downstairs to grab a bottle of water and a couple of aspirin, leaving them on his nightstand for her in the morning. He stared down at her for a few moments. Her mouth was open as she snored lightly. Her pushed back the hair from her face and trailed his fingers across her cheek. She was so beautiful, and he couldn't help thinking of that girl again, the sixteen-year-old version of Ashlynn who had stared at him with chocolate brown eyes so filled with hero worship he'd had a hard time not being affected by it. He'd never had anyone look at him like that, and he had to admit, he'd gotten a little carried away. He hadn't meant to hook up with Ashlynn in the back of his car.

He'd never meant to hurt her either. He'd always thought of her as a sweet kid who never caught a break. Everyone picked on her, and although she would always give back as good as she got, he'd found himself stepping in whenever he could. He'd never thought

26

anything about it until they'd been lying on the hood of his car, looking up at the stars and just talking.

And then she'd sat up and leaned over him, her hair falling around him as her lips had touched his.

Shaking himself out of his memories, he picked up the towel her clothes were wrapped in, flipped off the light and left the room. He shouldn't be thinking of that night. Hell, he hadn't really in twelve years since he left.

So why was he being haunted by it now? And why could he remember nearly every detail?

After throwing the pile of clothes into his brand new washing machine, and adding his shirt to it, he started looking for bedding. With a heavy sigh, he grabbed a blanket out of the box that was labeled hall closet and flopped down on his new couch.

As he laid back and closed his eyes, he tried not to think of the gorgeous woman sleeping in his bed, or their shared past.

One thought did persist, though.

Being the good guy fucking sucked.

***

The next morning, Ashlynn woke up with a moan, her mouth disgustingly dry and rancid. She squinted one eye at the sunlight peeking in through the blinds and closed it again, snuggling into the warm comforter. She could ignore the nasty taste in her mouth for a few minutes if it meant not having to get up out of the soft, silken sheets.

Her eyes popped open. Blinds? Soft sheets? She had curtains and her rough cotton sheets felt nothing like this.

27

Ashlynn sat up and looking around the room. Where the hell was she?

She noticed the bottle of water and two white pills. Whoever had brought her back to their place had left her alone in their bed and given her something for her potential hang over. The last thing she remembered was yelling at Sebastian Valentine and then vomiting all over his shoes.

Shit.

Pushing the comforter off, she realized she was in an oversized t-shirt and her underwear. Someone had undressed her and taken care of her after she'd gotten sick.

She picked up the bottle of water and chugged, silently praying it wasn't him. Anyone but Sebastian.

After she made a short trip to the bathroom, smoothing her hair and using some of the toothpaste on the counter on her finger to brush away the nasty taste from her mouth, she picked up her keys and her phone off the nightstand and left the room. She hadn't seen her clothes anywhere, but hadn't wanted to go through drawers to find pants either.

She slowly climbed down the stairs, and when she reached the bottom, saw a pair of bare feet hanging off the edge of the couch.

Tiptoeing around the couch, she looked down to find Sebastian's familiar dark head lying on the arm, his beautiful profile perfectly kissed by the sun pouring through the front window.

Crap. Damn. Shoot.

What the hell was she supposed to do now? The guy had taken care of her when she was sloppy drunk and let her sleep in his bed. Had taken the damn couch, and looked really uncomfortable doing it.

The knowledge was too much, and she did the only thing she could in the situation. She snuck out the door and closed it quietly behind her before taking off at a sprint for home. Ashlynn rushed inside, ignoring Bernie as he pushed his big head right into her crotch, and raced past him up the stairs. She flopped down her bed, and checked her phone for messages. A dozen text messages from Karianne and Maggie, all asking if she was okay.

Bernie's big tongue licked the bottom of her left foot and she squealed, "Bernie, damn it. Go lie down."

She caught the sad way the dog hung his head as he stared at her with big eyes.

Guilt gnawed at her stomach. "I'm sorry. Mommy is just grumpy. Come on."

Bernie leaped onto the bed and laid next to her, panting heavily, as if the small jump had been too taxing for him.

Dialing Maggie, she laid her cheek against her scratchy summer quilt with her face away from Bernie and ignored the way he snuffled her hair as she waited.

"I am only answering this early because I was worried about you." Maggie sounded raspy, and grumbly, but Ashlynn didn't care.

"Is there a reason why I woke up in Sebastian Valentine's bed this morning?"

"What?" Maggie's screech made her groan with pain.

"Too loud."

"Omg, did you sleep with him? Did he take advantage of you? I will murder him, straight up kill his ass—"

"Will you shut up? God, my head is about to split open. No, he wasn't in bed with me. He slept on the couch. He undressed me and put me in his bed with a bottle of water on the nightstand and left me alone."

"Wait, are you telling me you are calling me to complain that Sebastian Valentine took you home last night and did *not* seduce your panties off?"

"Of course not! What happened to killing him if he took advantage of me?"

Maggie coughed and groaned into the phone. "That was before I knew he'd been a perfect gentleman. Now I'm starting to believe Troy about him."

Ashlynn lifted her head up. "What do you mean?"

"That Bash had nothing to do with those pictures of you guys."

"Wait a second, since when is he Bash?"

"You should take a plate of cookies over and thank him for taking care of you," Maggie said, ignoring her query.

"Dude, no, and who the hell's side are you on?"

"The only side I'm on right now is my bed's, which needs me to get back to it. I'll talk to you in a few hours."

Before she could say more, Maggie ended the call.

Son of a bitch. If Sebastian hadn't been involved with the pictures, then she'd spent twelve years hating his guts for nothing?

Well, not exactly for nothing; he had taken off after their hook up and never called again.

Okay, but you two had hardly spoken before that night, except for the few times he'd stepped in and defended you. So, maybe he just thought it was something that happened and you weren't supposed to talk again.

Well, that was true. When he'd first been assigned as her science project partner, she'd been a little struck by how handsome he was. And nice. He was nice to her when no one else was, besides her close friends.

Not to mention that night, she'd been the one to make a move on him after he'd gotten her away from those jerks. He'd just been talking, that smooth deep voice like the sweetest melody, and she'd lost control, telling herself she might not ever get a chance like that again.

At first, he hadn't moved when she'd kissed him and she'd wanted to melt into a puddle and die. But as she'd pulled back, his hand had come up, cradling the back of her head, and he'd guided her back down to kiss him again. Only this time, he'd taken total control.

When they'd found themselves in the back seat of his car, she hadn't thought of anything but him. The whole experience had been messy, passionate, painful, and wonderful, all at the same time. He'd been so sweet and she'd been so glad she'd chosen him...

But then afterwards, the way he'd talked about leaving and the pictures the next day, her happy, romantic bubble had been brutally popped.

Except you're a grown up now, not some silly teenaged girl with her head in the clouds. Time to really move on and let go.

Climbing up off the bed, she decided that first things first, she needed to take a shower.

Then maybe she'd try out Maggie's cookie idea.

5

That evening, Bash emptied the last box of appliances in the kitchen, feeling pretty productive for a guy who hadn't woken up until almost noon. He'd had a stiff neck and back, but it was finding out that Ashlynn had snuck out the door without even a thank you note that had been really disgruntling.

After he'd taken care of her and given her his bed, she couldn't even have found a Post-it or something?

Someone knocked on his front door and when he answered it, he found Cate Sherman standing on his front porch with a casserole dish, her blond hair artfully framing her beautiful face.

"Hey, Bash. I figured you probably hadn't had a chance to shop yet, so I thought I'd bring you dinner for tonight. It's an enchilada casserole, so I hope you like spicy stuff."

Bash knew that Cate had ideas, which was pretty amusing since she'd never looked at him in high school. He hadn't played sports and picture-perfect Cate wouldn't have stooped to date a lowly mechanic's son. She'd been too busy chasing after the Sweet brothers, the four strapping heirs to Promise farms. Of course, considering she was still single, he was guessing none of those conquests had panned out.

Still, he wasn't one to say no to a free meal.

"Thanks, Cate." He took the dish with a grin. "I appreciate the neighborly gesture."

"Oh, well, sure." Bash could tell she was waiting for an invitation and when one didn't come, she gave him a very forced smile. "Well, I should get home. Lots of stuff to do."

"Sure, me too. Thanks again."

He shut the door, feeling a little bad. He wasn't trying to be mean, but the last thing he wanted was to hook up with someone from Promise when his life was in L.A. and he wanted to come back to Promise just to relax. Screwing around with any of the local woman would just complicate matters and he hated complicated.

Another knock sounded and this time when he opened it, it was Ashlynn, holding a plate piled high with cookies. Her face was scrubbed free of makeup and her brown hair was pulled back in a long ponytail.

Speaking of complicated.

"Hey, so, I made these for you. They're a thank you for taking care of me last night when I was such a mess."

Despite his resolve to not get involved with anyone from Promise, Bash found himself holding the door open wide. "You wanna come in?"

He watched her swallow nervously as she stepped over the threshold. "I don't want to disturb you, I'm sure you're busy…"

Bash's gaze followed hers to the covered casserole dish.

"I guess the welcoming committee already stopped by," she said.

"You wanna stay and have some with me?" Why the hell had he asked her that? Since he'd shown up yesterday, she'd been nothing but hostile and now she was standing there with cookies and he was asking her to dinner?

"If Cate Sherman made it, I think I'll pass."

Bash arched a brown at her animosity. "What did Cate do to you?"

"Besides being a horrible human being every time we see each other?"

"Well, she made the casserole for me, so I doubt it's poisoned," he said.

"It could be roofied."

Bash glanced at the casserole in horror and to his surprise, Ashlynn burst out laughing.

"Oh, my God, your face. Now you're actually considering it, huh? You think all the women here are just going to try to get into your pants 'cause you're a hot shot celebrity?"

Bash grinned sheepishly. "Maybe not my pants, but my shirt's another story. Speaking of which, I have your clothes. Do you have mine?"

Her cheeks flushed. "I tossed it in the wash, but forgot to transfer it on my lunch today."

"It's fine. Yours are on the end of the couch. I even got the puke stain out of your halter."

"Kill me now," she mumbled as she set his cookies on the kitchen table and went to retrieve her clothes.

"Doesn't sound like something I should do."

Ashlynn hugged her clothes to her chest as she turned around to face him. "Well, I won't disturb your night anymore."

"Ashlynn…" He waited for her to look him in the eye before he continued. "Do you remember anything I said to you last night?"

"No, not really."

"I told you that I wasn't involved in what happened after we…after we had sex. Do you believe me?"

She looked away from him as she answered, "Yes."

"Good. Then can we start over? Because I figure there are plenty of wedding preparations and events and I really don't want to spend them avoiding you."

"You don't have to. I'm fine, we're fine."

"Then it shouldn't be a problem for you to stay and have some casserole with me," he said.

***

Trapped. That was exactly how Ashlynn felt as Sebastian brought two plates over to the round kitchen table, one with a small square of casserole and the other with a large heap. He set them down, the littler portion in front of her, and walked back into the kitchen, rummaging through the drawers. She couldn't stop her gaze from straying down his back to his jean-covered ass.

Stop checking him out, you idiot.

36

She made sure she was looking anywhere but at him when he turned around and came back to the table.

"So, why did you decide to buy a house here?" she asked.

"I don't know. I have roots here, and friends. Just seemed like the right choice."

"Have you seen your dad yet?" The minute she asked it, she knew it was wrong. Sebastian stilled in mid-chew, and stared at something over her shoulder.

"No, not yet. Figured he's probably not that eager to see me, so why rush it?"

Silence stretched across the table as they ate. Ashlynn kicked herself for bringing up such a sensitive subject.

"I'm sorry you guys don't get along." *Stop talking about it.*

"It's not your fault. Was going on for a long time before things exploded."

"And you haven't even talked to him on the phone?" She just didn't know when to quit, and she blamed the healer in her...when she could see someone was in pain, she wanted to get to the root of the problem and fix it.

"Not even on the phone. I thought about calling a few times, but after the things I said to him, I figured he'd just hang up on me."

"I don't know about that. Most parents are pretty forgiving when it comes to their children," she said.

"Yeah, well, Samuel Valentine has never been the poster child for fatherly love."

She took a large bite of casserole before she said something else, watching him polish off his giant pile of green sauce, chicken, and tortillas. It made her sick the way some people could eat, and never feel any ill effects.

Well, not until later in life, anyway.

"So, you're a doctor now, huh? Your parents must be proud," he said.

Was he mocking her? "They are. Especially since I took over the clinic in town. They like that I moved back after medical school."

"Why did you? Didn't you want to work in a larger practice? Maybe be a surgeon in the city or something?" he asked.

"Not everyone feels trapped by the place they grew up."

Her words had definitely struck a nerve. He set his fork down on his empty plate and sat back, his muscular forearms crossing over his chest. "You're going to tell me that you actually like living here? After everything that happened to you?"

"There are shitty people everywhere. There are a lot less here than in other places. And I like working for myself, knowing all the people who come to my clinic." She stood up with her plate. "Besides, I don't have sex in the back of cars anymore."

She went to go set her plate up on the counter but his voice stopped her.

"Where do you have sex now?"

Ashlynn nearly dropped her plate. "What?"

She turned around to face him and caught the small smirk on his lips. "You heard me."

"And that's none of your business," she spluttered.

"I know. I just wanted to shake up the mood this conversation had going."

"You couldn't think of any way to change up the tone than to ask me about my sex life?"

He stood up, grabbing his plate, and came into the kitchen with her. The room seemed to shrink as he took her plate and leaned past her to set them both down.

She backed up until her butt hit the side of the sink, but he just kept coming. When he had her boxed in, he leaned over her and his lips teased up in the corners.

"What can I say? I find the subject fascinating."

6

Bash was playing a very dangerous game; one he'd already decided was a bad idea on every level. He'd just gotten to a civil place with Ashlynn, and here he was, putting the moves on her. If the last thing he wanted was to hook up with someone in Promise, then why was his mouth so close to Ashlynn's that he could feel the warmth of her breath on his lips?

Suddenly, her hands came flying up between them and she was shoving against his chest. "God, I can't believe I actually thought I was wrong about you."

"What?" He stepped back and she brushed past him.

"I thought that maybe I had misjudged you, that you were a decent guy. But you're clearly just a horny jerk looking to hook up with anyone."

"What in the hell are you talking about? I haven't hooked up with anyone—"

"So the first one you try out your charms on is the girl who gave it up so easy? I was a kid with a crush then. Now I know the difference between a hook up and something real."

"And you're looking for something real?" he asked.

"Damn straight."

She burst out of his house and he stood in the kitchen for a while, just staring off and thinking.

Bash had a life in L.A. and had no interest in getting serious about settling down. Besides, he figured when he finally did, it would be with someone who understood his job and all the time it took up.

Bash left the house right after her and found himself in his car, driving down the road toward Wilson's Garage. With any luck, he'd be catching his dad before his second beer, and maybe he'd be in a forgiving mood.

Not that his dad was completely innocent. He'd never gotten behind Bash's dream of leaving town and being an actor, telling him it was a bunch of foolish bullshit. That he needed to consider mechanic school, so when his dad bought Wilson's, he could rename it Valentine's Garage and pass it down to Bash when he died.

But Bash hadn't wanted his dad's life and when he'd told him that, rather colorfully, his dad had kicked him out and told him not to bother coming back.

Bash parked in front of the garage, surprised by the changes to the old cement block building.

Especially the name on the sign.

He climbed out of his car and headed for the stairs on the side of the garage that led to the upstairs apartment door. If his dad had

41

bought the garage, would he still be living here? He'd always told Bash that after his mom left, they didn't need much more than the two-bedroom loft, but if he owned the business, couldn't he afford a better place to live?

Bash knocked on the door and waited. Footsteps echoed inside as someone drew closer.

It opened up and his dad stared out at him, his eyes widening for a split second before his face snapped back into the familiar scowl he was famous for.

"Bash."

"Hey, pop. Sorry to drop by so late."

"Late? You mean late at night or twelve years late?"

Bash gritted his teeth at his dad's sarcasm. "You were the one who told me not to come back."

Bash noticed the tick in Samuel's jaw. "So why did you?"

Bash laughed bitterly. "You know what? I have no idea. I thought maybe you would mellow out in your old age, but I guess I was wrong. See ya."

"You're still a sensitive little shit, aren't you?" his dad called after him.

Bash stopped halfway down the stairs. "Yeah, I guess having a dick for a dad will do that to a guy."

Samuel seemed to be measuring him up. "Well, you drove all the way over here. Least I can do is get you a fucking beer."

He disappeared out of the doorway and Bash climbed back up the stairs and inside the apartment, closing the door behind him. It still looked the same, the dingy leather couch and stools at the counter where they'd eaten their meals.

Samuel came back into the room with two beer bottles and handed him one.

"Thanks. So, when did you buy Wilson's?"

"A few years after you left. Figured you'd need something to fall back on when being a star didn't pan out."

"Except it did pan out. I could retire now, and still have enough money for my grandkids to live on."

His dad didn't seem impressed. "Well, good for you."

Bash's skin pricked with anger at his dad's *la di fucking da* tone.

"You seriously can't be even a little bit proud of me? I mean, not very many people find the success I have. It's competitive as hell. That doesn't merit even a 'good job' from you?"

His dad took a long pull of his beer before answering. "Being paid to look pretty isn't like having a real job. It's not like you save orphans and shit from burning buildings."

Actually, in his movie *Heatwave*, he'd played a firefighter who had saved a bunch of orphans from a burning building. Had his dad seen it and was making a joke?

"Are you fucking with me?"

"No, why? Is it so hard to believe that not everyone wants to kiss your ass?"

Well, between his dad and Ashlynn, there were at least two people in the world who didn't seem to give a shit about what he did for a living.

43

"I don't need my ass kissed, but it would be nice to at least get a little encouragement for you once in a dozen years."

Samuel stared at him hard. "If you're looking for validation that you made the right life choice, you're not going to get it from me. You might have money, but from what I've seen on the television, you don't have much else. You got real friends in L.A.? Family?"

"Who are you to preach to me about family? You threw me out—"

Samuel's face turned an ugly shade of violet. "And you thought you were better than your old man. You forget that I was the one who stayed, who took care of you and raised you the best I could. But you were just like your mama, always thinking about yourself and your wants and needs—"

"Don't fucking bring her into this! This is about you and me, and how I didn't want to end up a bitter, lonely old man like you!"

Bash waited for his dad to throw one of his clenched fists, the only sound in the quiet apartment was their heavy breathing.

Then the front door opened behind Bash and he turned to find a blond woman who appeared to be in her mid-thirties come through the door balancing two grocery sacks, her obvious pregnant belly popping out in front.

"Hey, Sam, everything okay?" she said.

"Baby, I told you to call me when you got here and I would come down to get the bags." His dad pushed past him and took the sacks from the woman, dropping a kiss on her rosy cheek. "Now, sit your ass down and put your feet up."

The woman smiled so lovingly at his dad that Bash couldn't seem to find his voice. Then, she turned the beam on him and stepped forward with her hand out. "You must be Sebastian. I'm Jenna."

Taking her hand, he swallowed. "Nice to meet you. Sorry for all the yelling."

"That's okay, you should hear us go at it when your father is being a stubborn ass."

"I heard that," Samuel called from the kitchen.

"I meant for you to." She sat down on the couch with a groan and kicked off her shoes and socks. He noticed her swollen ankles as she put them up on the coffee table and when she caught him staring, she said, "Damn things won't stop swelling. Dr. Marks keeps following me around, checking my blood pressure. She's worried about preeclampsia, but I feel fine."

For the first time, Sebastian noticed she was wearing scrubs. "So, you're a nurse at the clinic?"

"Yeah, I usually work noon to nine to help get our night doctor up to speed on what happened during the day, but Dr. Marks is only letting me work from five to nine. She'd rather I was on bed rest, but I'm not ready to stop working."

"So…so you and my dad are…"

She held up her left hand. "I'm his wife. Going on two years." Jenna rubbed her stomach and said in a baby voice, "And this little girl is gonna be your sister, Virginia."

"Victoria," his dad said, sitting next to her and handing her a glass of water.

"Whatever, we're still deciding."

Bash was still trying to process exactly what was happening. His father, who had just turned fifty, was the father of this woman's baby? She was almost half his age!

"I'm sorry, but how old are you?" he asked.

He could see his dad tense up, but Jenna just laid a hand on his arm.

"I'm thirty-seven. Are you worried about our age difference?"

Bash's face burned. "No, it's just—I didn't know anything about you."

"Maybe if you'd called, you would have," his dad growled.

"The phone works both ways."

"I didn't know your number."

"You could have messaged me on Facebook or Twitter!"

His dad's lips thinned. "I don't mess around with all that online crap."

"You're right," Jenna jumped in, shooting his dad a warning look. "We should have figured out a way to get in touch with you. But you're here now. How long are you planning to stay?"

"I'll be here through my best friend's wedding at the end of the month."

"Perfect! My due date is July thirty-first, so it will give your father and you time to reconnect, and we can get to know each other."

Bash nodded, keeping his thoughts to himself. The biggest thing plaguing him was that Ashlynn had asked about his dad. She'd known he was married and his wife was pregnant.

And she hadn't even given him a heads up.

"Sounds good."

7

Ten days later, Ashlynn put the last of her camping gear into the back of her Jeep, checking over her list again. When Troy and Maggie had decided on a joint bachelor/bachelorette party that would be a weekend camping trip, Ashlynn had been stoked. She loved camping, and planned to do a lot of hiking during this one.

Which had nothing to do with trying to avoid the mouthwatering best man.

Since the night she'd run out of his house, he hadn't sought her out or tried to talk to her. She'd told herself that was a good thing, but unfortunately, a small part of her was still disappointed.

She headed back up her driveway to get Bernie and saw Sebastian walking out of his house, carrying a sleeping bag and a backpack. Was that all he was bringing for the whole weekend?

Oh well, it wasn't her problem.

He pulled out a few minutes before her and she found herself following that foreign little-penis car the whole way up and over the mountain. The campgrounds they were setting up at were right next to a swimming hole and several hiking trails. Karianne and Rebecca Warren, Maggie's cousin, had the first campsite, and Troy's two brothers had the second, and their tents were already up and in place. While Sebastian parked his car next to Troy's truck, Ashlynn pulled her Jeep into the last site before the curve. She waved at Troy and Maggie, who were standing in front of their overshot camper, and let Bernie out of the back.

Ashlynn laughed as Troy, seeing the big lovable beast, covered the front of his pants with a frying pan.

"You better not hurt my dog!" she yelled.

"Better his head than my boys!" he tossed back.

Maggie intercepted Bernie and gave the slobbering dog a big hug. "I second that. I'm gonna need those at a later date."

"Gross," Ashlynn mumbled.

She opened the back just as she heard Troy call out a greeting to Sebastian.

"Hey dude, is that all you brought?"

"No, I have an ice chest in the back with food and beer," Sebastian said.

"Yeah, but where are you gonna sleep? We're supposed to get thunderstorms tonight and tomorrow."

Ashlynn could see the confusion on Sebastian's face even from fifty feet away. "I thought I was bunking with you. This is a bachelor party right? I figured the girls would be in one campsite and us in the other."

Troy set the frying pan down and moved closer to say something softly to Sebastian. He nodded, and headed back toward his car.

"Where you going?" Troy asked.

"To go buy a tent somewhere."

"You don't have to do that, Bash." Maggie glanced Ashlynn's way before she continued, "Ash's got plenty of room in her tent, as long as you don't mind sharing with her disgusting dog."

How many times was she going to threaten to kill Maggie before she finally followed through?

"Naw, it's cool, I don't want to inconvenience you," Sebastian called.

Her choices were to let Sebastian go and waste another two hours or more trying to get a tent or be the bigger person and let him crash with her. It wasn't like her eight-person tent wouldn't fit them comfortably.

"It's not a problem. My tent has two separate compartments, so Bernie and I won't bother you." Sebastian hesitated, and she added in frustration, "Look, if you want to waste three hours driving back and finding a place that sells tents, go ahead, or you can man up and help me set up camp."

Catcalls and ooohs echoed from the rest of their group and Sebastian got back into his car and moved it next to her Jeep. He pulled out his ice chest first, while she opened up the back of her car.

Bernie came back and when he shoved his muzzle between Sebastian's legs, Ashlynn giggled as he pitched forward.

"Fucking dog, you got problems."

"He likes you. You should take it as a compliment," she said.

"He seems to like everyone."

"No, not really. He hates the FedEx guy."

She swore she caught a ghost of a smile on Sebastian's lips before his expression went stoic once more.

What the hell was his problem? All she'd done was reject him. Was his ego really so fragile he couldn't take a girl telling him she wasn't interested?

***

Once camp was set up, Bash went down to the bathroom to change into his swim trunks, giving Ashlynn the tent for privacy. He still wasn't sure what the hell to say to her about not giving him a heads up about his dad, but the sting of her silence was a little duller now. Turned out he really liked his dad's new wife. Even though things between the two men were still tense, Jenna was an excellent buffer. She was funny, and sweet, with just enough attitude to put his dad in his place. In fact, his new stepmother was quite the talker. She'd told him all kinds of surprising things about his dad, including the fact that they were saving up to buy a bigger place, apparently with at least four bedrooms because they wanted more kids.

And his dad seemed...happy. It was weird seeing him almost mellow in her presence. Bash could barely remember his mom, but when he did, it was always of the two of them fighting.

He walked back to camp, his flip-flops slapping against the dirt road as he went. He came around the side of her Jeep and picked up his ice chest just as she climbed out of the tent in a simple blue two-piece.

Holy fucking shit. He remembered the feel of her body when they were teenagers, the weight of her breasts in his hands, and although she was slightly slimmer now, she had the type of body that left him feeling eighteen again.

She caught him watching her and fiddled with the strap of the halter suit top, making her breasts push up even further over the top.

"Come on, you two! Daylights a wasting," Maggie hollered. She stood next to Troy in a white bikini and a black inner tube under her arm.

Ashlynn bent over and picked up a yellow and blue tube and a black canvas bag as she called her dog's name. Bash followed behind her, his gaze drawn to the sway of her hips. Her suit started to ride up a bit and he saw her right butt cheek peeking out the bottom.

It was a really nice view.

"What's in the bag?" he asked.

She glanced at him over her shoulder as she answered. "My medical kit. Epi-pen, antiseptic and sterile instruments in case I need to perform sutures."

"You have to do that a lot?"

"With this crowd? You'd be surprised."

He caught up alongside her, his bare arm brushing hers as they walked. He was trying to figure out how to bring up his dad to clear the air, but she beat him to it.

"I hear you met Jenna."

He glanced her way, but she'd slid a pair of black polka dot sunglasses over her eyes.

"Yeah. Thanks for the heads up, by the way," he said.

"Sorry, I didn't know if it was my place to tell you."

"No, I get it, although at the time, I was pretty pissed," he said. "Turns out I like Jenna better than I do my old man."

She flashed him a smile. "Yeah, Jenna is great. Really good with the patients and knows how to put them at ease. I just wish she'd take care of herself, too. I've been trying to get her to go out on maternity leave and she won't."

"Have you mentioned it to my dad?"

"No offense, but your dad still scares the crap out of me," she said.

Bash laughed good-naturedly. "Tell me about it."

They reached the sandy beach and Bash set his cooler down at the line of trees.

"You want a beer?" he asked.

"Not yet." She pulled a bottle of spray on sunscreen and held it out to him. "Can you spray me down?"

Bash couldn't help wishing she'd brought the lotion he'd need to spread all over her with his bare hands.

Once she was coated, she took the bottle from him and aimed it at his chest. "Your turn."

"I'm good. I don't burn."

She arched a dark brow at him, her full lips twisted mulishly. "As a doctor, I am going to advise you to let me cover you so you don't end up with skin cancer and ruin that handsome face with deep gouges from having carcinomas removed from your nose and cheeks."

"You think I'm pretty vain don't you?"

"Your face is your job, isn't it? Let's go."

He didn't like the reference; it was too close to what his dad had said about his career. As she sprayed him with the mist, he thought about what he could say to her that wouldn't make him sound whiny.

"You know, acting is more than what you look like. You have to remember your lines, work long hours, and I do a lot of my own stunts, so I have to be in peak physical shape."

"So I've noticed," she murmured softly.

He looked over his shoulder at her and her cheeks lit up pink at his grin.

"I also get hurt. A lot. And I have to be on point for interviews and always watch what I say so it can't be taken out of context later. Believe me, it's no cake walk."

"Then why do it, if it's so rough?" she asked.

Bash turned to face her, his gaze locking with hers.

"Because it's what I love."

He watched her chest rise and fall as she breathed, the world around them dropping away as he took a step closer, drawn to her by those big brown eyes.

Cold water sprayed them, and Ashlynn jumped toward him with a cry. He caught her to him just as another stream hit him in the side of the head.

"Get in here, bitches!" Troy yelled from his inner tube, a Super Soaker in his hand and trained right on the two of them.

Bash vowed sweet revenge on his friend for cock blocking him.

Then again, he did have his arms wrapped around a laughing Ashlynn, holding her warm body against his.

Maybe Troy had done him a favor after all.

8

Ashlynn, wrapped in her cozy wool sweater and black sweatpants, sat in her folding chair next to Bash later that night, not even trying to stop her knee from brushing his. Somewhere during the day she'd stopped thinking about him so formally as Sebastian, and started calling him Bash. It suited him better, anyway.

All day their group had romped and played in the water, but she'd found herself more than once with her arms around Bash's neck or hiding behind him as one of Troy's brothers shot a stream of water her way.

And he hadn't seemed to mind. In fact, he'd held onto her in the water for a long time, his strong arms wrapped around her middle, and she could feel him pressing against the back of her. There had been no denying he liked being there, if the hard-on had been any indication, and she was having trouble remembering that he was only here to visit. This was a vacation from his real life, and she didn't want to be just a distraction again.

"Your marshmallow is burning," he said.

Ashlynn realized that he was right and brought it out of the fire swiftly, blowing on it rapidly. The whole outside was charred.

"Shit. At least it will be gooey."

"Here." He took her pole from her and gave her his perfectly browned one. "I like mine well done."

The warm yellow and orange flames cast shadows across his face, lighting up his eyes in the dark and her heart swelled involuntarily at the gesture.

"You don't have to do that," she protested.

He put the burned marshmallow on his graham cracker and chocolate without answering. Then, he placed the other cracker on top and smushed it between his fingers before he took a big bite, some of the white marshmallow and chocolate sticking to his lips as he chewed.

"Mmm, so good," he said.

Laughing, she created hers and took a bite. The sweet smoky flavor was heavenly. She moaned around her mouthful of s'more and Bash chuckled.

"Are you two making love to your s'mores? 'Cause those noises you're making sound hella dirty," Karianne said.

"I think they're warranted. S'mores are totally orgasmic," Maggie said.

"Dude, whose idea was it to go camping with chicks? Men don't talk about orgasms around a campfire," Troy's brother, George said.

"I think it's kind of hot," his other brother, Cliff chimed in.

Troy leveled his brothers with a lethal stare across the fire. "That's my fiancée you're talking about. Don't make me kill you."

A rapid-fire discussion ramped up about how his two older brothers could totally take him, but Ashlynn was too distracted by the white sticky smear on the top of Bash's lip.

Before she could stop herself, she reached out and removed it with the tip of her thumb, gliding it across his rough stubble.

She started to pull away and he caught her hand, bringing it to his mouth. As his tongue slid across the pad of her thumb, she shivered and squeezed her legs together.

Someone clearing their throat brought Ashlynn out of her aroused state, and she turned to find several sets of eyes staring at them with expressions of surprise.

Ashlynn jerked her hand away and stood up. "I'm going to bed."

She didn't even wait for the round of goodnights to finish or for Maggie to follow her to question what was going on. Calling Bernie, she unzipped the tent and dived in.

Turning on her lantern, she found her pajamas and changed quickly, afraid Bash would come in any minute.

She went to the bathroom and brushed her teeth before climbing into her sleeping bag. Every noise outside the tent made her jump, until finally, the unmistakable sound of the zipper opening the front of the tent sounded.

Ashlynn heard the rustle of Bash's clothes being removed behind her, and an image came over her of him when he was eighteen, all lean muscle and washboard abs in backseat of his car. His hand sliding over her hip as he angled her up and the tip of him rested against the juncture of her thighs.

"Are you sure?"

She'd whispered yes, and wrapped her arms around his shoulders, hanging on tight as he'd slipped inside her for the first time.

Oh, God, can you just stop thinking about sex with Bash when he's only a few feet away from you?

"Ash? You awake?" he asked, softly.

She tried to keep her breathing even, pretending to sleep, and after a few moments of rustling, the sound of his snores reached her ears.

Ashlynn closed her eyes and tried to sleep, but all she kept thinking was what a freaking coward she was.

You're just protecting yourself. If you get involved with him and he leaves in two weeks, you're going to hate yourself and him. Again.

But she still wanted him, no matter how logical she tried to be about it. Wanted his smile aimed at her, his deep blue eyes watching her in that appreciative way, just like he had earlier today. She wanted his hands touching her everywhere and his lips...

God, she wanted to kiss him so badly it was like a physical ache.

No, she was already in danger of falling for him. Underneath the egotistical action star was a good man, a gentleman who took care of people, who cared about them even as he pretended to be hardened.

Yeah, she could definitely fall for a guy like that.

***

The next morning, Ashlynn woke up just as the sun was coming up and decided to hike to the top of Heaven's Peak to watch the sunrise. She changed into her hiking boots, jeans and a t-shirt, zipping her black sweatshirt on over it. She packed a backpack with water bottles, a bowl for Bernie to drink from, and climbed out of the tent, calling Bernie softly. She tried not to wake Bash as she rezipped the tent and grabbed a couple of Cliff bars and dog bones from her snack bag.

She waited a minute or two, listening for stirring inside the tent, but thankfully, he didn't get up. She said a little prayer of gratitude. She'd had a restless night and was not ready to see him before she had a clear head and at least one cup of coffee.

She brushed her teeth and used the bathroom before setting off with Bernie. The trail was quiet except for the twitter of birds and the soft breeze rustling the branches. It hadn't stormed like they'd thought it would last night, but there were puffs of white clouds in the sky, lined with orange, and pink from the rising sun.

Bernie panted along beside her as they climbed, the trees thinning as they drew closer to the top.

Ashlynn's mind wandered back to Bash. Why couldn't she just enjoy their little flirtation without letting feelings get in the way?

60

She could just hook up with him. After all, it had been a while and she'd slept with him before. What was the big deal?

Because she just couldn't. She liked him, despite her every effort not to. And letting things go too far was just going to sink her deeper. When he left, she was going hurt again, and it would be all her fault this time.

The toe of her sneaker snagged on something and she pitched forward, catching herself on her hands. Sharp rocks bit into her hands painfully, and she cursed.

This is what you get for not paying attention and mooning over Sebastian Valentine again.

She started to climb to her knees, avoiding Bernie's tongue on her face with a laugh.

"I'm okay, Bernie, stop."

As she pushed Bernie's big head out of her way, she saw something in the underbrush a few feet away move. A tan head with two golden eyes that were watching her with intent. She saw the shoulders wiggle as the long tail twitched in quick swings back and forth.

It took Ashlynn too long to realize she was looking at a cougar.

Bernie's head whipped away from her, and she knew the minute he noticed the large cat. She reached for his collar too late.

"Bernie, no!" she screamed just as her beloved dog charged the crouching cat with a series of booming barks and growls.

Instead of running, the cat challenged the dog, its high pitched scream turning Ashlynn's blood to ice as she struggled to get her pack

61

off. If she could reach her bear spray, maybe she could scare the cat off.

Bernie let out a yelp of pain and Ashlynn glanced up in time to watch the cougar's giant claws swing through the air and connect with her dog's shoulder.

When the dog backed away, the cat took off, disappearing into the brush.

"Bernie, stay."

She didn't bank on him listening and lunged for his collar, but she realized she had miscalculated where the cougar had sliced him. A large puddle of blood was edging out under Bernie's feet and she could feel the warm wetness running against her knuckles.

The sound of heavy footsteps behind her spooked her and she turned swiftly.

Bash rushed to her side before she could even react.

"What the fuck happened?"

9

Bash had woken up to the sound of someone outside and when he'd realized it was Ashlynn and her dog, he'd decided to catch up to her and talk to her alone. He wasn't sure what had happened at the campfire last night, but he knew damn well she hadn't been asleep when he'd come to bed.

He watched her head up the edge of the trail, keeping a little distance between them. He didn't want her to escape before he'd talked to her.

When he'd heard her scream for her dog, he'd run up the trail at full speed, his calves protesting the steep incline, until he'd spotted her kneeling on the ground, holding her dog's collar, her face devoid of color.

It wasn't until he kneeled next to her that he'd seen the pool of blood mixed in the dirt, seeping into her jeans.

"Ashlynn, answer me. Are you okay?"

"Bernie. A cougar was over there and Bernie went after it."

"But you're okay?" he repeated.

"Yes, I'm fine."

"Then let's get your dog back to camp. Do you have his leash?"

Bash could see the shake in her hands as she pointed at her pack. "In there."

Bash retrieved it and latched the leash. He prayed the dog could walk, because carrying a hundred and fifty-pound dog down the steep trail was going to be a rough endeavor.

Bernie limped along beside Ashlynn, leaving a trail of blood behind them. It took them longer to get down than it had taken to climb up, and Bash could tell that the dog was hurting. As the trail leveled out a bit, he bent down and lifted the dog into his arms. Bash carried him back to camp while Ashlynn ran ahead to start the car.

Bash made it back with the dog in time to find George running toward him with Ashlynn close behind. He knew George was a large animal veterinarian, so it only made sense that Ashlynn would ask for his help.

"Heaven's Peak Veterinary Hospital is the closest and I know Dr. Robins is open Saturday. I'll go with you guys to show you the way," George said.

Bash nodded and when they reached the Jeep, Bash said to Ashlynn, "You get into the back and I'll lay him on your lap. You're in no condition to drive."

To his surprise, George climbed into the back seat with Ashlynn and Bash had no choice but to gently place the dog across their laps with their help.

"This way I can hold pressure while you talk to him," George said to Ashlynn, as if Bash wasn't even there.

Ashlynn held out the keys to Bash, her attention focused on her dog as she spoke to him softly. Trying not to take it personally, Bash climbed into the driver's seat, feeling like a chauffeur as he pulled out and followed George's directions.

"Thank you, George. I'm glad you were here," Ashlynn said from the back seat.

Sure, I carry the dog and get nothing, but good old George gets a thank you for being a human Garmin.

"You're welcome, but Jocelyn would be more help in this situation," George said.

"Who's Jocelyn?" Bash hadn't meant to ask, but he didn't like how close George was sitting to Ashlynn.

"My girlfriend. She runs the small animal side our veterinary practice in Promise."

Hearing that George had a girlfriend relieved some of Bash's tension, until he realized why he'd hated the thought of Ashlynn fawning all over George.

He was jealous. He didn't want Ashlynn interested in another man, in something real with someone else.

God damn it, he liked her. When in the hell had that happened?

They pulled into the parking lot of Heaven's Peak Veterinary Hospital thirty minutes later and Bash took the dog from them, his gaze meeting Ashlynn's tear-filled eyes.

"I've got him. You get the door."

He let her and George go first, and walked into the waiting room as George was talking to the receptionist.

"He's got three gashes along his shoulder and neck."

"George, is that you I hear?" a deep voice called from out of sight.

"Yeah, Craig, we got an emergency out here."

A burly guy with a trimmed beard and fucking man bun came out of the back in a white lab coat. Bash watched him check out Ashlynn before turning his attention to Bernie in Bash's arms.

Before he knew what was happening, the giant handsome hipster had taken Bernie from him and George and Ashlynn were following behind, disappearing through the double doors.

"Oh my God, you look just like Sebastian Valentine!" the receptionist cried.

At least somebody didn't think he was completely forgettable.

***

An hour later, Ashlynn came out of the back alone, the adrenaline slowly seeping out of her. George had offered to stay behind with Dr. Robins while he stitched up Bernie, who he said was a very lucky dog. George assured her that Dr. Robins would drive him back to the campsite later, so Ashlynn should go back and try to have fun. She could pick Bernie up tomorrow and he would be in good hands until then.

But how was she supposed to just forget about everything that had happened this morning? The fear and the helplessness. She'd never felt that before—she had always been in control.

Actually, that wasn't true. She'd been in a situation where there was nothing she could do to stop it or fix it.

She walked through the double doors and found Bash leaning over the counter, that killer smile on his face.

He was flirting with the receptionist. While she was scared and miserable, he was feeding his ego?

She let the doors slap closed behind her loudly, and Bash glanced her way, not even bothering to act ashamed.

Why should he? You aren't together and he doesn't want you to be.

"I'm ready to go," she said.

"Alright. Hey, Rita, it was nice to meet you."

"You too, Bash. I can't wait to tell my brother I met you."

Ashlynn couldn't stop herself from mimicking her under her breath, but the woman was oblivious.

Not Bash though. He was fucking grinning at her.

The bastard.

They got outside to the Jeep and she held out her hand. "Give me the keys."

"Are you sure? You seem a little geared up to be driving—"

"Give me the freaking keys before I destroy you."

He tossed them to her as he went over the passenger side and climbed in. She started the car before he was buckled and took off, speeding down the dirt road with a vengeance.

"Whoa, speed racer, what's your problem?"

"You are my problem. I mean, do you have to flirt with everything? As long as it has a pair of tits? You just can't help it?"

She saw him grinning out of the corner of her eye and her foot pressed down on the gas.

"Are you jealous?" he asked.

"Of course I'm not jealous. I'm upset because my dog was nearly killed and I was scared for my life and I just—"

"Pull over. Now."

The sheer boom in his voice was enough to break through some of her hysteria, and she did as he asked.

Once she parked and killed the engine, Ashlynn jumped in surprise as he unbuckled her seatbelt.

"Get in the back," he said.

He got out of the Jeep and climbed into the back seat.

"What are you doing?" she asked.

"Just get your ass back here before I drag you over the seat."

Ashlynn wasn't really worried about his threat, but something about the tone in his voice spurred her to do his bidding.

When she was finally seated next to him, he wrapped both of his arms around her and held her against his chest.

"Now, if you need to be mad at me, you can be, but for the record, I was just being friendly. I wasn't flirting."

She let out a choked laugh, surprisingly calmer in his embrace. "Same difference."

"No, you see, when I flirt, it's with intent. I do it because I want to take a woman home or get what I want from her. When I'm being friendly, then there's nothing more than pleasant conversation and a smile."

"Do you flirt with me?" she asked.

"I'm always flirting with you."

His words kick started her heart at a gallop. "Then what do you want from me?"

His hand slid under her chin and she let him tilt her gaze up to his.

"I wish I knew."

10

Bash woke up to the sound of rain pounding on the roof of Ashlynn's Jeep, and her slow, even breathing puffing against his chest. When had they fallen asleep? The last thing he remembered was them talking about how Jenna and his dad were still arguing over the baby's name.

He looked out the window, and it was darker outside, but he couldn't get his phone without disturbing Ashlynn. Bash figured it didn't matter when they got back since the rest of their friends were probably hanging out inside their campers and tents. He stroked the side of Ashlynn's cheek and thought about everything he'd discovered today, things that got him thinking about what he was going to do when his next part came through.

He hadn't wanted to complicate his life, but the minute Ashlynn had flipped him the bird, he hadn't been able to get her off his mind. He'd tried avoiding her, but there was no denying the pull she had for him. Even when they'd been younger, he'd wanted her, but it was different now. He was thinking like a man, a man who had a giant house in a posh neighborhood in L.A., with more cars than he had time to drive, and yet, nothing else to show for all of his wealth. He couldn't even remember the last time he'd been camping like this, just chilling with friends. He couldn't remember the last time he was *actually* happy.

Of course, he could have done without the blood and terror, but at least that had made him feel something.

He enjoyed the money and the fame, but not the way he had at first, when he'd been a poor, small town kid eager for the spotlight. As much as he loved his job, he didn't know if he could go back to his old life of parties, women, and solitude.

Here in Promise he had friends. He had family.

And he had Ashlynn.

"Mmmm." She stretched against him and when her arm almost clocked him, he laughed. She opened her eyes and smiled up at him. "Sorry, I was tired."

"I can see that. It's alright, I was just listening to the rain."

"What time is it?"

Now that she was up, he reached into the middle console for his phone and checked the time on the screen. "It's a little after one."

"Oh, man. Everyone's going to wonder where we are."

"Nah, they're probably too busy to worry about us," he said.

"Maggie and Troy maybe, but Karianne and Rebecca and Cliff are probably bored out of their minds."

"Or…" Bash wiggled his eyebrows suggestively. "Maybe they found a way to occupy their time."

"Oh, gross, I do not want to have that mental image flashing through my mind." She scooted away from him toward the door and he was more than disappointed when she said, "We should go. George will be back soon with an update on Bernie."

"Yeah, good old George."

Ashlynn paused with her hand on the door. "Are you jealous of George?"

"What, just because the guy swooped in and put your mind at ease and saved the day by knowing the local vet? Nah, why would I be jealous."

To his surprise she slid back over and planted a kiss on his cheek. "But, he didn't come to my rescue when he heard me screaming or carry Bernie back to camp when he couldn't walk anymore. You did."

"Well, to be honest, I was already following you when I heard you yelling Bernie's name."

"Oh? I didn't hear you. Why were you doing that?" she asked.

"Because I wanted to know what was going on with us. Last night, it seemed like we were connecting and then you got spooked and took off."

"I already told you, I'm looking for something serious, not temporary," she said.

"And I don't know what I want, but I do know it starts with you. I like you, Ash, and I want to explore that."

If he wasn't being completely clear, he cupped her face in his hands and kissed her, his mouth sliding over hers gently. No pushing, just coaxing a response from her.

He didn't expect her to take a hold of his biceps and open her mouth under his, allowing him access to her tongue. They danced together, breathing heavily, and Bash's hands slid down her throat, gliding over her chest to span her waist.

Bash was shocked as hell when Ashlynn pulled back enough to take off her sweatshirt and t-shirt, leaving her in just a simple white sports bra.

"Okay. Explore me."

**

Ashlynn knew she had just taken the rulebook and all her common sense and tossed them right out the window, but she didn't care. She was tired of worrying about how she was going to feel when Bash left or if she was going to end up just as brokenhearted as the first time.

She couldn't go another minute without feeling every part of him against her.

Bash helped her out of her sports bra before his lips closed around first one nipple, then the other. She threaded her fingers into his hair as he made love to her with his mouth, her legs trembling with need.

He brought his hands up to cover her breasts, his lips finding the slope of her neck.

"I thought you didn't do it in cars anymore?"

He dragged his teeth across her sensitive skin and she gasped, "I guess you're the exception."

His deep chuckle vibrated against her sensitive flesh and she shivered.

While their hands tore at each other's clothes, baring inch by inch to hands and lips, Ashlynn closed her eyes and listened to the tap of the rain, the rhythm of it making her body move against him until the last barrier was discarded.

She heard the rip of a condom and slowly opened her eyes, a sly smile on her lips.

"You thought you were going to get lucky this weekend?"

"Only in my dreams."

"Ugh, that is a cheesy line," she said.

"Shut up, I'm under pressure. As in, if I don't get inside you now, I'm going to fucking explode."

Her laughter was smothered by his kiss as he lifted her over his cock and flexed up into her as he held onto her hips. She moaned as he filled her, pressing down on him as he set her in motion, rocking her up and down on his length until she felt her muscles hum. The pressure built between her legs as the rain continued to pound, and he started moving fast, manipulating her until she was gripping his shoulders, releasing high, keening noises with every hard thrust.

When her orgasm broke over her, she threw her head back, lights exploding behind the lids of her closed eyes as she screamed. He kept moving, torturing her sensitive body in the best possible way until he finally jerked against her, his arms squeezing her waist as he groaned.

Ashlynn held onto the seat behind him and rested her forehead against his.

"I totally take it back."

"What's that?" He was gulping in air, his chest heaving against hers.

"There is something about sex in the backseat that is so fucking hot."

11

A week later, Ashlynn woke up in Bash's bed alone. Since the afternoon in the back of her Jeep, they had spent every free minute together, a lot of them in bed. He'd even made an appointment right before her lunch at the clinic and they'd ended up playing a game of "dirty doctor" that had left Ashlynn dreamy eyed and smiling the rest of the day. The week had felt like a month, and the more she got wrapped up in him, the harder it was to think about him not being there.

She sat up and called Bash's name, but there was no answer. Bernie was lying on the floor by her pile of clothes, his head barely lifting. Ashlynn thought it was sweet that Bash had started letting Bernie crash too, since that way she didn't have to get up in the middle of the night to go home and let him out to pee.

Ashlynn frowned down at her dog, though, as he started rolling on top of her clothes. They'd been in such a hurry to get naked when she'd come over after work, she hadn't been concerned about black fur covering her white tank top and jean shorts.

She climbed out of his bed with the sheet wrapped about her torso, taking the stairs quietly as she listened to Bash talking to someone.

"Well, yeah, that is a great part, but could they hold filming until the first of August? I've got a few personal obligations to handle before I leave Promise."

Obligations? Did he mean the wedding, or the birth of his baby sister?

Or did he mean telling her it was over?

Her foot touched the landing and the floor squeaked beneath her, alerting him to her presence. He glanced at her over his shoulder and held up a finger.

"Yeah, I'd appreciate it. Thanks."

She smiled at him despite her racing thoughts as he turned around to face her.

"Hey, good news?" she asked.

"Yeah, a fantastic part. Let's just hope they can be patient." He took the few steps that separated them, and kissed her lingeringly. "Have I mentioned how hot you look in my sheets?"

"No, but considering this is the first time I've worn them, I'll let it slide."

"Mmm, thank you." He nibbled on her neck, and she giggled.

Bernie clomped down the stairs behind them and her mirth intensified as Bash pressed tighter against her and Bernie tried to shove his head between them.

"Seriously, your dog's obsession with crotches is disturbing."

As much as she just wanted to laugh and be in the moment, the fact that they had only a week left until Troy and Maggie's wedding was weighing on her. The last week had been a whirlwind of shared meals, going out with friends, and of course, wild, hot romantic sex.

But as the time drew closer to an end, she couldn't help wondering what it would mean. Would Bash be done exploring what they had, or would he decide to stay? To make it work?

After all, how were they supposed to have a relationship if he was off every other month playing a movie hero and kissing some of the most beautiful women in Hollywood as his costars? How was she supposed to keep him interested when he had all that going on the minute he left Promise?

Bash's phone rang again and he pulled away reluctantly, seeming oblivious to her mood.

"Hey, pop." Ashlynn watched Bash pale as he gripped the phone to his ear. "I'm on my way."

"What's wrong," she asked. "Is Jenna okay?"

"She started feeling bad last night, so he drove her to St. Luke's in Ketchum. They're taking her in for an emergency C-section now."

"I want to go with you. Jenna is a friend and I want to be there." She raced up the stairs as fast as her sheet clad body would take her, finally dropping it and racing buck naked for her clothes on the floor. She pulled them on in record time and came back down, tying her hair up into a ponytail.

"Okay, I'm ready."

Bash, still standing in his boxer shorts, quirked his mouth up into a little half smile.

"I tell you what. You go home and change, and I'll swing by to get you in a minute?"

Her skin started itching and she looked down at her fur-covered body. She'd totally forgotten about Bernie snuggling and rolling his hair all over them.

"Yeah, probably a good idea. Just don't leave without me."

***

It took thirty minutes to reach the hospital and another fifteen to figure out where they needed to go. A nurse finally directed them to where the waiting room was for labor and delivery. Bash rounded the corner with Ashlynn hot on his heels and found his dad sitting, cupping his face in his hands.

"Pop, what's going on?"

His dad looked up, his face gray, and Bash's heart sank.

Ashlynn touched his shoulder. "I'm going to see what I can find out."

Bash went to sit next to his dad on the couch, resting a hand on his old man's shoulder. "Pop? Tell me."

"I don't know. The C-section went fine, and they took the baby down to the NICU because she was a few weeks early, but they said she looked great. I stayed with Jenna as they moved her into her recovery room, but when the nurse came in to check her a few minutes ago, she acted weird, like there was something wrong. She kicked me out of the room and then I watched six other nurses rush in after her."

His dad looked at him with red-rimmed eyes, and Bash realized his dad was weeping. "I can't lose her, too. First your mom walked out, and then you. I can't lose Jenna. I love her so much."

Bash wrapped his arms around his dad, and let him break down against him. It made Bash realize for the first time that maybe he had been more of the problem than his old man. He was the one who had been ashamed of their little apartment above the garage and the fact that they didn't have a lot of extra money. Bash had worked his ass off to save money for his car in high school and clothes that didn't come from the Goodwill.

He remembered the times he'd blown his dad off when he'd wanted to show him how to do something on a car, how he'd wished that his dad could understand and respect his dreams. Now he realized he'd never done the same for his dad. He'd made his dream of owning a shop seem small time and stupid, but it had been everything to him.

And now, his dad might be losing the only person he thought understood and loved him for who he was.

It was surprising that for as much as they butted heads, Bash never realized he and his dad wanted the same thing.

Acceptance.

Hugging his dad tighter, he whispered, "She's gonna be okay, pop. You'll see. She's gonna be fine."

Ten minutes later, Ashlynn and a tall man with a head of thick dark hair came into the room.

His dad seemed to recognize him. "Doc, is she—"

"Mr. Valentine, your wife and baby are fine. Your wife had some excessive bleeding, but we were able to stop it before it became critical. She'll be weak for a few days, so we'll probably keep her one more day in the hospital, but we'll wait and see how she feels."

"Can I see her?" Samuel asked.

"Of course, follow me."

Bash and Ashlynn walked along behind Samuel and the doctor, and when Ashlynn reached out to take his hand, he was grateful she was there.

They waited in the doorway as Samuel rushed in and leaned over a pale Jenna, brushing her blond hair off her forehead.

She opened her eyes slowly, and gave him a small smile that nearly undid Bash.

"Hey, handsome. I didn't worry you, did I?"

"Woman, I love you, but if you ever scare me like that again, I won't be able to take it."

Her hand covered his. "I'll do my best."

When his dad laid his head on his wife's chest and he saw those big shoulders shaking again, he pulled Ashlynn out of the room.

"We should give them a few minutes."

"Of course."

Her tone was distant, and he glanced her way. "You okay?"

"Yeah, I was just thinking about how lucky they are. Finding a love like that."

Bash didn't know what to say to that, so he just pulled her into a hug, resting his chin on the top of her head.

***

Ashlynn watched Bash holding his new little sister, rocking her gently as he paced his stepmother's hospital room. Samuel sat in a chair next to Jenna, holding her hand, and Ashlynn felt a little left out, as if she was intruding on a sacred family moment.

"We've definitely decided on a name," Jenna said.

"Oh, yeah?" Bash asked.

"Yep. Candace. Do you like it?" Jenna asked.

"I do."

Ashlynn's heart squeezed as she imagined a completely different scene involving just the two of them, her sitting up in the hospital bed while he paced around her room, holding their baby while they argued over names.

Oh, God, you cannot think like that.

But it was too late. It hadn't taken long at all for Ashlynn to realize that when she saw her future, it was filled with fantasies about Bash. Bash mowing their lawn, taking Bernie for walks, and pushing their children on the front swing in his yard. Their yard.

Because against her will, she was already in love with him.

What the hell was she going to do now?

12

Ashlynn smiled as her best friend and her new husband came into the barn at Promise Farms, beaming at each other. The barn was beautifully decorated with white, twinkly lights and round tables surrounding a sawdust dance floor.

Bash stood next to her holding a microphone. It was time for their toasts, and although they had worked on them at the same time, neither one knew what the other would say to their friends.

Troy and Maggie took their seats at the head table and once everyone had settled, Bash started talking.

"For those of you who don't know me, I grew up with Troy and he was the best friend I've ever had. Which is why I'm so glad he found a woman just as genuine, funny, and kind as he is. I wish you both a lifetime of happiness and hope to someday find what you guys have. A love worth waiting for."

His words sliced through Ashlynn and she tried so hard to keep a smile on her face as she took the microphone and cleared her throat.

"Maggie and I have been best friends since infancy, and the thing I feel completely confident in is the fact that Troy loves her more than anything and she him. These two people would move heaven and earth to be together and I know that nothing will ever separate them. To Maggie and Troy."

Ashlynn tossed back her glass of champagne and quietly snuck outside, just needing a moment of air.

She and Bash had spent another blissful week together, visiting with Jenna, Samuel, and the new baby, Candace, and at one point, she'd watched Samuel and Bash step outside and talk. When they'd come in, Bash had been in an unbelievably good mood and when they'd arrived back at her place, he'd made love to her with so much passion and joy, she'd nearly blurted the words.

But last night, she'd stopped by his place to find his bags packed and waiting by the door.

"You're not leaving yet, right? The wedding is tomorrow."

"No, I'm taking off afterwards. Just saving time."

He'd tried to get her to stay, but she'd made up an excuse about Karianne coming over. Then, she'd called Karianne and asked her to come over and stay so she wouldn't do something stupid.

Too bad stupid had officially left the building.

"There you are," Bash said, coming up along the side of the barn next to her. "I wanted to talk to you before I leave."

Ashlynn wiped at her eyes, trying to avoid his gaze so he wouldn't see she'd been crying. "It's okay, Bash, you don't have to say anything."

"What do you mean? What's wrong with you, you act like I'm leaving forever." He cupped her face in his hands and brushed her tears away with his thumbs. "I'll be back."

"For how long?" she asked.

He shrugged so airily that it set her teeth on edge. "I don't know, until the next project, I suppose."

"And until then I'm just supposed to wait? To hope that you remember to call?" She reached up and pulled his hands away from her face.

"I'm going to call, Ash, and we'll figure it out."

Ashlynn shook her head, needing to get everything out before she lost control and believed him. "No, you told me that acting was the only thing you loved. Well, I need more than that. I need a man who loves and needs me more than anything. Even his career."

Bash lost his confused smile and he stiffened. "Are you asking me to give up my career?"

"No, of course not. But I'm also not going to play second fiddle to it, either."

Before he did something that might weaken her resolve, like kiss her, Ashlynn ran toward where her car was parked, kicking off her heels as she went. Even when she heard him calling her name she didn't stop.

There just wasn't anything left to say.

***

85

After a week being back in L.A., Bash had come to a decision about his future and about Ashlynn. He'd tried to call her every day since he left Promise, but she wouldn't return his calls. The first few days, he'd been furious with her for thinking the worst of him again, and was about to say to hell with her.

But then he'd started thinking about John, who'd convinced him that if something wasn't hard, then it wasn't worth having.

So, he'd started shifting his priorities, beginning with his home in L.A. He didn't need a million-dollar home in California when he planned to spend most of the year in Idaho.

Next, he sat down with his agent, letting him know he'd be slowing down his project load for a while. When he'd started to protest, Bash had reminded him that he worked for him and that he still promised to take on the high budget films his agent loved. That had certainly smoothed some of the rustled feathers.

Now, he just had to make it through the next month and get back to Ashlynn before she did something stupid, like give up on him.

13

Ashlynn wiped at her eyes again, trying to hide the fact that she had been crying for the thousandth time. In the last month, she'd made all kinds of excuses for why she had red, puffy eyes, or a runny nose, but everyone had just given her pitying looks.

God, she was so tired of the pitying looks.

Picking up the chart on the outside of the door, she knocked once before stepping inside. "Hello, Mr....Valentine." Her head jerked up and sure enough, Bash was sitting on the edge of the patient table, looking way too handsome.

"Hey."

"What are you doing here?" she asked.

"I've got this terrible pain in my chest that I just can't seem to get rid of."

"No, not at the clinic. What are you doing in Promise? I thought you got this huge part and you just couldn't turn it down."

"I do, but I have a couple days and this couldn't wait, so I took the first flight I could get to Sun Valley. Of course, you'd know that if you bothered to answer any of my phone calls."

Ashlynn blushed hard at his chiding and had a hard time deciding whether she was happy or frustrated he was back. "But you told me that when you left you wouldn't give up acting."

"I'm not and I won't. This is my passion, and it's what I want to do." He hopped off the table and took the chart from her, setting it down on the table. "But it's not what I love. Not anymore."

Ashlynn sucked in her breath as he cupped her hands in his. "I love you, Ash. If you can accept me, all of me, I want to give what we have a shot. I want to spend my days and nights with you, and when I'm working, I want your voice be the first and last I hear when I'm sick with loneliness for you."

She tried to pull her hands back, fighting tears, but he wouldn't let her go.

"How would we make that work when you'd be gone half the year doing movies, and I'm here?" Ashlynn cried. "It's not like I could follow you around the world, I can't leave my practice or my patients—"

"I'm not asking you too. And it wouldn't be half the year. I'm going to slow down and be very choosy with the parts I take. One or two roles a year, and the rest of the time, I'll be right here in Promise, following around the prettiest girl next door I've ever seen."

The tears won and spilled over, trailing down her cheeks. "It sounds so easy when you say it like that."

"It is, I swear." His hand cupped the side of her face and when he dipped his head to kiss her, she let him. When he pulled away again, he was smiling down at her. "Now, I'm going to go out on a limb here and guess that the reason you've been avoiding me and acting crazy is because you love me too, and thought I was going to ditch you again."

"Maybe."

Laying his forehead against hers, he whispered, "If I promise that I will never leave town without telling you, the woman I love, will you please let me take you to dinner?"

Ashlynn wrapped her arms around his waist and laid her head on his chest. "I'd like that."

"Good. Now, about the pain in my chest…"

Ashlynn smiled as she pulled away to gaze up into his beautiful blue eyes. "Can you show me where it hurts?"

He moved his hand between them and laid it right over his heart. She lifted his hand and pressed her lips there.

"All better?" she whispered.

"Getting there."

She stood up on her tiptoes and kissed his neck. "How about now?"

"You know, I've got several places that could use your attention, doc," he said, a devilish glint in his eyes.

Ashlynn slowly lifted her arms up, releasing her hair from its clip. Shaking her wavy length around her shoulders, she grinned as his hands gripped her hips hard.

"You know, I'll have to examine you quite thoroughly," she said. "You should probably take off your clothes."

Bash released her and stepped back, lifting his shirt over his head, and her mouth ran dry as he revealed every delicious inch of his torso. His hands went to the button of his pants and he raised his eyebrow.

"Aren't you going to lock the door, Doc?"

Blushing, Ashlynn went to do just that, turning in time to watch Bash slip his boxers down to his ankles and step out of them.

"So, I've got ouchies here," he touched his shoulder, "here," the right side of his six pack, "and here." His hand gripped the base of his cock and he slid his hand all the way down to the head.

"Well—" Ashlynn slid out of her lab coat and kicked off her shoes, "I guess we'd better get started."

Acknowledgements

I would like to thank my very patient editor, Rebecca, for working with me on this. My agent, Sarah, who supports me in all I do. My husband and children, for understanding when I'm on deadline and loving me anyway. The rest of my large, crazy family for supporting me in this journey. To my friends, both in the business and out, who don't mind listening to me when I need to talk and being there when I need a break. For my Rockers, who kick some serious buttowski. And to my amazing readers, who keep sticking with me. I love your guts.

Discover More by Codi Gary

Rock Canyon, Idaho Series
The Trouble With Sexy
Things Good Girls Don't Do
Good Girls Don't Date Rock Stars
Return of the Bad Girl
Bad Girls Don't Marry Marines
Bad For Me

The Men in Uniform Series
One Lucky Hero
Hero of Mine
Holding Out for a Hero

Coming Soon:

Hot Winter Nights Series by Codi Gary and James Patterson
A Bear Mountain Rescue Story

About Codi Gary

An obsessive bookworm, Codi Gary likes to write sexy contemporary romances with humor, grand gestures, and blush-worthy moments. When she's not writing, she can be found reading her favorite authors, squealing over her must-watch shows, and playing with her children. She lives in Idaho with her family. Codi loves hearing from her readers, so be sure to visit her at http://codigarysbooks.com, Facebook: CodiGarysBooks, and Twitter: @codigary.

CPSIA information can be obtained
at www.ICGtesting.com
Printed in the USA
BVHW01s1917260218
509140BV00009B/310/P